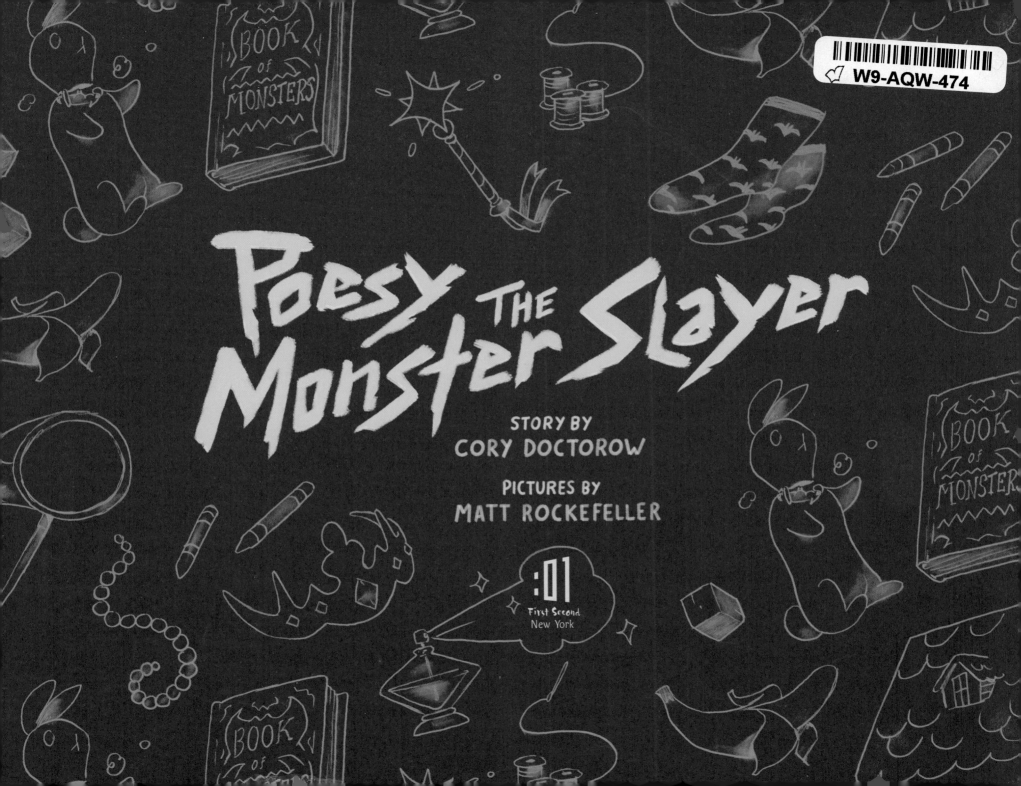

# Poesy THE Monster Slayer

STORY BY
## CORY DOCTOROW

PICTURES BY
## MATT ROCKEFELLER

:01
First Second
New York

Poesy, bedtime!
Monster LaIr!!!
Parents! Always with the bedtimes!

Poesy knew she should sleep, but she was MUCH too excited.

She'd been listening to the spooky noises and watching the shadows. She knew the monsters were coming, but that was okay. She'd been doing research with her monster book.

She'd been MAKING PLANS.

A werewolf! Poesy knew all about
werewolves from her monster book:
*hungry, raiding backyards by moonlight,*
*snatching birds from the nest.*

SSHNG!

Werewolves HATED silver,
and they feared the light.

Poesy waved her wand. The wolfman whimpered at the zigzags of light.

She leapt from the bed, collaring the werewolf with her Princess Frillypants silver tiara. He rattled the window with his howl and scampered off with his tail between his legs.

Victory!

Daddy was cross.

You are supposed to be in bed and asleep. You are NOT supposed to be playing with toys.

He took the wand out of her hand, tucked her in, and went back to bed.

Sorry, Daddy.

Poesy didn't tell him about the werewolf.

Poesy didn't stay in bed.

Daddy was scared of monsters.

Let DADDY stay in bed.

Great Old Ones were hard to miss, once you knew what to look for—like a family of octopuses all tangled together. They pounced like CRAZY.

Poesy had heard this one climbing her bookcase that evening. This was gonna be FUN.

The Great Old One made a noise like a frightened teakettle in a blender rolling down a hill.

She sprayed her bubblegum perfume in its terrible lidless eye, and it slithered away, crying.

Mummy looked REALLY scary.

YOU GET INTO BED RIGHT NOW.
It is nighttime. It is dark outside.
I am asleep. Daddy is asleep.
YOU GO TO SLEEP!
HOO HOOO HOO HOO

Poor Mummy was so tired.

Poesy would have to take care of the rest of the monsters more quietly.

First up: vampires. They really hated to get dirty.

Good thing Daddy left her a midnight snack!

As the vampire ran for the laundry room, Poesy tripped it with her necklace.

It changed into a bat!
Poesy caught it in a net
made of fairy wings.

SKREE!
SKREE!

Poof

TP
TP TP

Wrrrrr

It turned into mist! Poesy turned on
her fan and blew it out the window.

POESY EMMELINE FIBONACCI RUSSELL SCHNEGG!

Poesy was SURE she'd been quiet, but Daddy had ears like a bat.

He was so tired that he stepped on a Harry the Hare block and said some swears. Poor Daddy!

Rotten monsters!

Good thing there was only one left.

Frankenstein's monster sounded scared and sad.

Frankenstein's monsters are ALWAYS losing their heads.

They don't mind, they're used to it.

And luckily, Poesy loved
to make new toys.

Some monsters were tougher than others.

She'd do battle with the zombies another night.

:01

First Second

Published by First Second
First Second is an imprint of Roaring Brook Press, a division of Holtzbrinck Publishing Holdings Limited Partnership
120 Broadway, New York, NY 10271

Don't miss your next favorite book from First Second! For the latest updates go
to firstsecondnewsletter.com and sign up for our enewsletter.

Library of Congress Control Number: 2019903651
ISBN: 978-1-62672-362-7

Our books may be purchased in bulk for promotional, educational, or business use.
Please contact your local bookseller or the Macmillan Corporate and Premium Sales Department
at (800) 221-7945 ext. 5442 or by email at MacmillanSpecialMarkets@macmillan.com.

FIRST
EDITION

First edition, 2020
Edited by Calista Brill and Rachel Stark
Cover and interior design by Jen Keenan
Printed in China by RR Donnelley Asia Printing Solutions Ltd.,
Dongguan City, Guangdong Province

Drawn with Mitsubishi Hie-Uni pencils and graphite powder on
Fabriano 90lb Hot Press watercolor paper and colored digitally in Photoshop.

1 3 5 7 9 10 8 6 4 2

BY ART
WE LIVE